Five Little Ducks

illustrated by Penny Ives

Child's Play (International) Ltd

Ashworth Rd, Bridgemead, Swindon, SN5 7YD UK

Swindon   Auburn ME   Sydney

© 2002 Child's Play (International) Ltd   Printed in Heshan, China

ISBN 978-0-85953-447-5   HH220410BH8X806104475

791086

www.childs-play.com

Five little ducks went out one day,

Over the hills and far away,

Mother Duck called, "Quack, quack, quack, quack!"

Four little ducks went out one day,
Over the hills and far away,

"...k, quack, quack, quack!"
...ducks came back.

Three little ducks w

Over the hills and far aw

Mother Duck called, "Quack, quack, quack, quack!"
But only two little ducks came back.

Two little ducks went out one day,
Over the hills and far away,

Mother Duck called, "Quack, quack, quack, quack!"

But only one little duck came back.

One little duck went out one day,
Over the hills and far away,

Mother Duck called, "Quack, quack, quack, quack!"
But NO little ducks came back.

No little ducks went out one day,
Over the hills and far away,
Mother Duck called,
"Quack, quack,
quack, quack!"

And five little ducks came wandering back!